THE

EXCITEMENT

I

BRING

2

WARREN C. HOLLOWAY

"AMERICA'S NEW STORYTELLER"

GOOD 2 GO PUBLISHING

THE EXCITEMENT I BRING 2
Written by WARREN C. HOLLOWAY
Cover Design: Davida Baldwin, Odd Ball Designs
Typesetter: Mychea
ISBN: 978-1-947340-54-1
Copyright © 2020 Good2Go Publishing
Published 2020 by Good2Go Publishing
7311 W. Glass Lane • Laveen, AZ 85339
www.good2gopublishing.com
https://twitter.com/good2gobooks
G2G@good2gopublishing.com
www.facebook.com/good2gopublishing
www.instagram.com/good2gopublishing

ONE

5:49 p.m.

Jaelen was pulling into the Pinehurst Estates ready to have his private in-home class with his client Laila Patrones. He was focused not just on a good workout, but getting into her head and heart space in order to figure out what was needed to access the financial information about her and her husband. He already knew that the $2,274.56 wasn't enough to get her through the week with her lifestyle. He and his associates viewed this as a dummy account since there were only cash deposits made, no electronic deposits, which would give them an idea where the money was coming from.

As he was driving up to her home he noticed that she was also approaching her home, jogging up to her 7,500-square-foot mansion boasting five garages, six baths, three half baths, two fireplaces, and a crystal chandelier greeting its visitors in the foyer with the white marble floor with traces of gold in it, game room, home theater and more.

As he was pulling up, Laila noticed his truck closing in on her home. Her jogging came to a slow before she walked up to his truck that stopped on the outside of the driveway.

As his window came down, her face shifted from slightly upset about him being late, because she thought he wasn't going to show, to a smile when she saw his good looks and smile he was greeting her with.

"I hope you can forgive me for my lapse in time. I was caught up with some other things," he said. She glanced down at her watch, seeing that she'd been running for close to twenty-five minutes.

"You can still come in," she said, walking up the slanted driveway. He was looking at her ass as she took each stride pushing her way up the driveway toward the front door. He wanted her in every way. He was even having thoughts of going all in with her to appease himself as well as to lock her in, so he could figure out how to access her financials.

The truck came to a halt, and he turned it off before he exited with his workout bag and mat.

"I was beginning to think my money wasn't good enough for you to make this house call. That's why I took off jogging to get myself in shape."

"I try to give all my clients the respect and attention they need and deserve. Even if they don't know they need or deserve it," he responded, with his word play getting her to look over her shoulder back at him before she unlocked the door. He followed behind her, taking in all of the fine amenities of this sumptuously furnished home. "Where would you like me to set this stuff up at?"

She turned around and faced him, looking into his eyes with this look that seemed to pull him into her space.

"Where would you like to work my body out at?" she asked, playing with her words. He was almost at a loss for words, being caught off guard by her word play. Thoughts of her husband being out of town raced through his mind as he processed this convenient house call.

"We can start right here until you

decide we need more space. Then we can shift to another room," he responded, knowing she was playing with him. This mansion had a gym and he knew it, because most mansions do, even if the owners never put it to use.

He placed the mat on the floor then started pulling out small two-pound and five-pound pink and blue dumbbells. There was also a red eight-pound medicine ball he would use for the stomach and leg exercises.

"First we're going to hit the legs, tightening up the hamstrings and glutes.

Then we'll hit the abs. You already did the cardio, jogging."

"We can do as much cardio as you like; my body needs it," she said, flirting with him and giving off a brief smile before lying on her stomach.

He took the medicine ball and placed it between her ankles.

"Keeping hold of the ball, lower it then bring it back up. You should feel it immediately in your hamstring and glutes. Your stomach should also be contracting with each rep." She started to exercise. "Two more then lower the ball to the floor but hold onto it for the next set," he said, squatting down beside her placing his hand on the back of her thigh. "You should have felt the burn right here; then it goes up to right here," he said, touching the top of her butt then the side, pointing out the target areas.

"I felt it on the inner part of my butt too," she said as her hand came around touching the area where she felt the burning. His eyes followed, wishing his fingers could be that close, but he wouldn't feel like that was being professional.

He knew what she was doing. He would play along until she gave into him without hesitation.

"Give me another set," he said, instructing her. She did as she was told, running through the set, followed by a few more. "Okay, that's enough of that. Turn over so we can hit those abs." She obliged, turning over and adjusting her tight yoga pants, displaying her curves and passion print. In his mind, looking on at her body of perfection, he wanted to be intimate with her in every way. She could see this in his eyes, making her smile, loving the tease.

"I'm ready for this ab workout," she said, getting his attention.

"This is going to be a real belly burner. Get into the crunch position, hold the ball by your knees, put your hands behind your neck to assist you in the crunch. Okay, give me twenty like this," he said.

She started feeling the burn right away. He was pointing out the areas she should feel it: her belly, the sides, even the thighs.

"Damn, this burns," she let out after the set.

"The things we go through to get what

we want," he said.

"That's easy for you to say with a body like that and having good genetics," she said.

"I didn't wake up like this. Then again, today I did. Damn, I'm blessed," he said, making her laugh at how silly he was.

"So, what's her name?" Laila asked, catching him off guard with the question.

"Who?"

"The lucky woman who has your attention. The one that falls asleep at your side every night?"

At first, he thought she was talking about Tanya. Then he realized she was fishing for answers to see if he was single. This was a question of interest.

"She is beautiful, her eyes lure me in each time as if they're speaking to me. Oh, and her body, I could be close to all night and day. The scent of her sweet perfume lingers, and I can see her when I close my eyes, as if she's near."

"Aww, that's so sweet. What's her name?" she asked.

He held his index finger up continuing to speak. "The best part about her is she's driven. She captured my attention from day one and has had it ever since. But I can't have her as I please." He stopped right there leaving her to think of his every word but wanting to know her name and more about her.

"Why can't you have her as you please? And what's her name?"

He leaned over her getting close and looking into Laila's eyes, then shifted, moving closer to her ear, and whispered, "I can't have her as I please because she's married." Hearing him say this, her heart started beating fast as her mind was processing what he was saying. "As for her name, it's Laila Patrones. She's a rare beauty like a butterfly. One has to capture greatness before it vanishes." His lips brushed lightly up against her ear as her heart was fluttering from his words.

His face caressed hers as she let out, "This is so wrong," in a low yet sensual tone as if wanting to resist what was next. However, it came faster than she could resist, his lips finding hers. Her heart pounded feeling his tongue moving into her mouth, tasting sweet and minty from the Icebreaker's candy. Her lips melted into his. He could feel his heart racing too, because part of what he said to her he genuinely meant. Her arms wrapped around him pulling him closer. She loved what was taking place, as if all of the resisting him was paying off. Her body was heating up as his masculine hand found her breast and pressed up against it, turning her on, a light moan vibrating over his tongue. She didn't want her first time with him to be here like this with her sweaty body; she would save that for another time. She lightly pressed up, pushing him away as her lips came off of his and their eyes locked. She wanted more, and he wanted her just as much. Their breathing had picked up. "I can't like this. I want to take a hot bath. I'll run up to the master bedroom and start the water. I want you to go to the lower level and get the bottle of pre-mixed apple martini. You can get whatever you like."

He helped her to her feet.

"I'm looking forward to getting drunk off your juices and berries," he said. She smiled, raising up on her toes and placing a kiss to his lips before turning around and making her way up the steps. He was looking on at her, taking in her beauty and imagining all the things he was going to do to her and with her.

He headed downstairs as she directed him, to make his way to the bar area. As he headed toward the bar, he walked past an open room that looked like a study. He halted in his tracks as business overrode all sexual thoughts, especially with tens of millions on the line. He took a step back and looked into the office, seeing a computer, hard drive, and more. His mind started racing, getting this rush as he entered the room and quickly went over to the computer and tapped the keys, trying to access the code. Nothing. Then it came to him: lift the keyboard up. He did just that. There was a name, but it was faded from the movement of the keypad. He zoomed in trying to make out the name. At the same time his cell phone sounded off sending a jolting fear through him and making him drop the keyboard. He took hold of his cell phone and saw it was Monty reaching out to him. This was business, so he answered, speaking lowly.

"Tell me something good, Monty."

"Why you talking in your sexy bedroom voice, fool?"

"I'm in her house trying to access info on the computer, that's why."

"I found out who he met at the airport. I'm sending you her picture. Her name is Farah Cantrelle; she's a model from Italy."

Hearing her name triggered Jaelen's vision of what he had seen on the bottom of the keyboard. He flipped it up and saw the faded name. "That's it," he thought.

"Gotta go. Hit me up in a few hours," Jaelen said, hanging up and accessing the computer using Farah's name. As soon as it went through, Jaelen shook his head knowing they never would have figured this out. It was stupid for Laila's husband to write the password down like that. Now he was going to pay big time. It didn't take long before Jaelen figured out how to get into his accounts. There were millions in multiple accounts. Close to seven million. This was even bigger than Tanya. In fact, this got him even more excited than the potential sex he was going to have with Laila. He took a picture of all of the account numbers, so he would have access no matter where he was in the world. Then he shut the computer down and put everything back as it was. He rushed out of the study over to the bar and secured the bottle of apple martini along with glasses and a bucket of ice. Then he took a bottle of Patron Silver for himself, before heading up stairs.

TWO

As he made it to the top of the steps, he could smell lavender as he got closer to the bathroom. It was game time. He was thinking, knowing he had to do everything in his power to make this all come together. No more teasing one another, but he wanted to remain in control, allowing her to know who the sexual dominant was.

He came to the door of the master bathroom and saw her standing on the outside of the tub with bubbles layering the top. The scent of lavender stimulated his senses just as much as seeing her goddess-like body stepping into the bubble bath.

"I'll celebrate a body like that any time," he said, getting her attention to his presence. She turned and looked over her shoulder as she continued getting in the tub. Her hair was down, adding to her nude sex appeal. He made his way over to the countertop by the his and her sink. "One apple martini for the lady in the nude jumpsuit," he said, making her laugh.

"That's cute and funny," she said, looking on at him and wanting more of his kiss and touch.

He poured the martini from the glass with the ice into the empty cup, giving the drink a proper chill before taking it over to her.

"Enjoy, beautiful," he said, handing her the drink.

"Thank you for the drink and those soft kisses downstairs," she said, giving him this look with lustful eyes. There was something else in her eyes too. He just couldn't figure it all out, which made him gravitate toward her even more. He poured himself a double shot of Patron Silver before coming back over to her sitting on the edge of the large tub. She was halfway done with her drink, he noticed. He downed his double shot before standing back up.

"Finish that off so I can make you another before I come back over to keep you company and have a nice intimate conversation."

"Bossy, huh? You like being in charge?" she asked before finishing her drink as requested.

"Bossy, no, in charge or taking control of one's heart, mind, and body, allowing them to escape pain and come into my world of pleasure and excitement, yes," he said, turning to make the drinks. She was looking on at him turned on by his assertiveness. She wanted him to take charge of whatever was to come tonight, she was thinking as she washed with the sponge.

He made the drinks and returned to her side.

"I want to toast to you and I unleashing our desires on one another and making this night one to always remember," he said with his eyes locked on hers looking deep into hers as if to caress her heart and mind with his words. She was all for it, smiling back at him before sipping her drink.

"Wash my back, please," she asked, wanting to be the first to initiate control. He obliged, downing his double shot, which felt warm going down his throat, adding to the first double shot that was streaming through his veins giving him a nice buzz.

She handed him the pink sponge, and he took it, grazing the bubbles on top of the water before placing it against her back and washing her shoulders, then her back, before going down lower to the small of her back. He extended his finger and touched the crease of her bottom. This intrigued yet teased her, wanting his fingers to go further. His hand came back up, around to the front of her body and over her perky breast. He tweaked her pink nipple and then continued over her belly. He started going lower until she halted his play.

"That's not my back." He paused, looking into her eyes and then at her lips, seeing how flush and plump they were, desiring him to go further yet she was resisting him. He smiled, releasing the sponge and taking his hand down further and placing it between her legs. However, he did not touch her place of passion, but she thought that was where he was going.

"Sometimes we have to show people want they want in order for them to know that they even need it or deserve it," he said. He removed his hand and stood up, making his way back over to the bucket of ice. She looked on at him hoping she didn't run him away. Then as he turned with the bucket of ice, she knew that there was going to be more to come. He took a few pieces and placed them into his mouth, then a few more in his left hand that she didn't see. He closed in on her placing the bucket down and leaning in to place a chilled kiss to her lips. She welcomed it, especially as his ice-cooled tongue made contact with hers allowing her to get the rest of the ice in his mouth.

The flavor of Patrón mixed with apple martini over their tongues added to this intimate kiss. He brought his left hand around allowing the handful of ice to make contact with her back. She jerked and moaned, vibrating her tongue over his. It was shocking but turned her on when his left hand came around and slid the handful of ice over her flesh until he reached her breast. "Mmmmh," she moaned, feeling her already tweaked nipples rubbing up against the chilled ice cubes. He pulled back from the kiss and lowered himself to the breast he was rubbing ice on. His lips took in her cooled nipples only to make them warm with his tongue. Her breathing picked up as she looked on at him working his tongue over her breast and nipples. Thoughts of other places she would like his tongue entered her mind. At the same time his free right hand dived under the bubbles closing in on her place of passion. He parted her legs, finding her perfectly waxed paradise. He placed his thumb up against her clitoris rubbing in a circular motion creating a sensation that made her moan. "Aaaah, Jae; aaaah, Jae; aaaah." Her moans picked up the faster his thumb circled her pearl. His tongue left her breast and found her neck, kissing it before nibbling on her neck, shoulder then back up to her ear. She was overwhelmed by his touch from every angle.

"Aaaah, Jae. Okay, hold on. Mmmmmh." He stopped all movement and leaned back taking a look at her. "Get in the tub with me," she pleaded before taking her glass of apple martini and drinking the rest of it while watching him remove all of his clothing. For the first time she was able to see all of him from head to toe. "You look like a Greek god, Jae," she said, never having been with a black man, or someone as fit as he was. He stepped into the oversized Jacuzzi-style tub that could fit three to four adults comfortably. Now he was at her side, they resumed play. She extended her hand, caressing all of him. Her heart pounded, knowing she'd crossed the line long ago having him enter her bathroom, and now sharing the tub. His length was more than she'd ever encountered, which also placed some fear into her, never having anyone outside of her husband since she'd been married. He welcomed her touch on every part of his body. He parted her legs, closing in reaching out, raising her body up. She was thinking about all of him about to enter into her tightness. Instead he reached down and removed her hand, taking hold of himself and rubbing it up against her. She let out a moan as her head went back. "Mmmmmh, don't tease me," she let out. He wanted to keep going, but he wanted this part first.

"How bad do you want it?" he asked. Her head came back up as her eyes opened.

"We can stop right now if you like," she said, switching it back around on him. He didn't want that. He wanted all of her just as much as she wanted him inside of her.

"Wrap your arms around me and hold on tight. Close your eyes and lean your head back," he instructed her, raising her body up and preparing to allow her to receive all of him. He could feel her embrace gripping tightly as her breathing was picking up anticipating his thickness and length finding her body. He took his right hand and reached up her back, grabbing a fist of her hair. She let out a light moan, shocked and turned on at the same time. Then it happened: he lowered her body down slowly onto his pulsating hard magic stick that was filling and stretching her V. She felt the passion as she slid down on him.

"Oooooh, Jae; ooooooh Jae; mmmh, mmmmmh." She was moaning, feeling her hair being pulled as he was stroking deep into her body at the same time lifting her up and down with his left hand. Her tight grip around his neck was also assisting in her riding him hard and fast, feeling the pressure that was creating intense pleasure she'd never felt before. "Mmmmm, Jae, mmmmmh. What are you doing to me? Mmmmmh." She let out a heated moan and sigh as she was going up and down. He was loving the feeling of her body too. This was beyond what he had expected. In fact, a part of him was falling for the idea of being with her in the long run, which made him hold on to her hair even more, hating the idea he was having because it would go against everything he and his friends had planned. "Aaaaaah, my body, Jae, I feel my body exploding inside, mmmmmmh, mmmmmmh." She let out moans that escalated the more the soaring of butterflies moved around inside of her as the powerful orgasm was building reaching its peak of explosion that she could no longer hold back. "Mmmmmh, Jae, let my hair go, Jae." She was moaning, feeling the intense pressure of powerful passion racing through her body making her want to lean in to be more intimate with him. Her moans stimulated his mind as he started thrusting harder, faster, side to side, deep and deeper into her body. "Oooooh, hold me, Jae. Mmmmmh, hold me, Jae. Mmmmmmh, oooooh, ooooooh." He let her hair go feeling himself closing in the moment of explosion. He continued thrusting hard and deep. Her lips were against his neck now, breathing heavily in between nibbling on his ear. "Mmmmm, I can't believe this is happening. Mmmmmmmh," she let out, feeling overwhelmed and turned on so much by what was taking place. His movement was still fast and his manhood was pulsating, becoming firmer as he reached his peak of eruption. She could feel it tightening inside of her as he went faster. This was making her cum even more. She bit down on his neck embracing the next wave of orgasms. He didn't mind because it was turning him on, stimulating his mind and enhancing his thrusting into her body.

Here it came; he couldn't hold it back. He didn't want to have control over the moment. He wanted all of his control to be given to her in this very moment. She assisted his eruption, going up and down on him until he came to a slow halt. Her intense moaning and biting on his neck stopped. She raised from his neck and came around to his lips, placing a kiss on them. Strange as it was, this moment felt like they'd done it before, almost like they had been lovers for some time with how effortless this was and how it felt to the both of them. She swayed her hips a little more getting more of him. "I can get used to this every day, Jae, especially the hair thing. You caught me off guard with that, but I like it because it did something to me."

"Like I said, some people don't know they need to be somewhere until we take them there," he said, moving his hand down below to her bottom and pressing his thick index finger up against her asshole.

"Aaaah, no, no," she let out, taken back that she even liked that.

He smiled, kissing her lips. He stood with her still in his embrace and stepped out of the tub before walking into the bedroom and laying her on the California king-sized bed with red and black silk sheets. He placed another kiss to her lips before whispering, "I'm going to cherish this moment, appreciating your body as God designed it be catered to," he said, allowing his kisses to trail from her lips to her neck, down to her tweaked breasts, over her belly that was flinching at his touch. Then he came face to face with the art of her pretty kitty. He placed a kiss on it, thinking about the seventeen million reasons he was pulling out all of the stops. He parted her vaginal lips and came close with his tongue and finger, caressing her pearl before thrusting his tongue into her body. She started squirming, sliding across the silk sheet, until his arms secured her legs and body in place. He continued his oral magic, making her moan and breath heavier, the faster his tongue and fingers moved in, out, and over her body.

"Jae, mmmmmmmh, mmmmmmmh, this feels so good, mmmmmmmmh." Hearing her moan, he introduced his index finger back to her asshole, pressing up against it, creating a euphoric pressure filled with pleasure.

"Oooh Jae, Jae, Jae, oooh, mmmmmmh, no, no, no, mmmmmmmmh." She was moaning trying to resist the intense power of orgasms that were soaring through her body back to back the more his tongue enter her body backed by his fingers being strategically placed on her pearl and bottom. "Jae, mmmmmmh, mmmmmh. I can't, I can't, mmmmmmmh, mmmmmmmh." She was moaning and breathing heavy, unable to hold the ultimate orgasms back anymore. He could feel her body shaking as each orgasm was racing to be freed from her flesh. She tasted sweet to him, making him want to enjoy her love spot all day. He came to a slow halt, thinking about his next step since her body was now sensitive to his touch. He stopped his tongue play, releasing her legs, only to wipe his mouth and coming up close to her as his left hand took hold of his manhood and pressed up against her super-sensitive love spot, entering her slowly. She wrapped her legs around him and pulled him close, wanting to embrace this moment he was giving her that felt like he was making love to her body as if they had been together for many years. This was exactly what he was doing to achieve what was needed. At the same time part of him wanted her to be in his future, somehow, someway.

Her lips were close to his ears unleashing heated breaths as her moans faded to this orgasmic heat escaping her mouth. He whispers into her ear as he was going deep, side to side, in and out making her feel so good. "I want to cum when you cum, baby," he said, turning her on even more, making her flow rush through her body. He could feel her V contracting on him, which triggered that feeling inside of him, making him pick up his pace until they each reached the simultaneous eruptions, making this intimate session even more unique. Their motions came to a slow halt before she unwrapped her legs and her embrace, allowing the two of them to look into each other's eyes.

"I really thank you for being good to my body. You made me realize what my husband is lacking, which is everything." She let out laughing before getting back to their time. "No, I can say I love what just happened and how my body feels thanks to you."

"I guess you brought the best out in

me, because your body feels good and tastes good to me. I look forward to more of you."

"More? What if this was all I wanted?" she said, looking on at him for his reaction.

"Oh, I get it. You got what you wanted out of this."

"Did I?" she responded, pausing before continuing on. "What's more important to you, the prize or the reward?"

He was caught off guard by the question because he didn't know what she was talking about exactly, yet the question came with intrigue.

"It depends on what the prize and reward are. If they're one in the same, then I choose both. If the prize is you, then it's what I choose."

"That's cute. I'll keep that in mind when I'm craving more of you," she said, smiling. Then she added, "We're not going to be all weird about this at the gym, are we?"

"I'll conduct every class as I normally do. I respect your space and position as a married woman; besides, I want to have a chance to keep claiming my prize," he said, making her laugh.

They continued talking and having intimate sessions that led to more open emotions and thoughts being spilled from each of them. This night became far more than either of them expected. It was around one in the morning when Jaeden finally left Laila's place feeling good about the intimate session as well as the conversation he and her had in between. Thoughts of including her in his life now seemed real as they discussed her leaving her husband, but for now she would hang in there until they figured it all out. If Monty and SK knew how their best friend was falling into this emotional situation with Laila, they would be pissed, because in this business they're in love, and the likeness to love is dangerous when they're the ones falling into it.

THREE

The next day, 11:07 a.m.

Jaelen was at his place still under the covers in a comfortable sleep. He was holding on to his pillow thinking it was Laila next to him, not realizing he'd left her place in the middle of the night. However, the intimate session they had shared made him connect with her while draining him to the point he'd overslept his normal weekend wake-up time, which was eight in the morning, so he could go running before he started his day. Lost in the dream state he could feel Laila's lips on his, her warm body close yet intimate. He could even smell the lavender of her bath water.

His cell phone on the nightstand started going off followed by text message alerts that pulled him out of his dream state. He opened his eyes and turned over toward the sound of the ringing cell phone. He rubbed his eyes, zooming in on the time of the Google clock, and saw how late it was compared to his normal wake-up time.

"I can't believe this shit." He sat up in bed and looked at his phone and saw how many calls and text he had missed. He had missed calls from Monty, SK, Tanya, and Paula. The messages he missed were from Danna. She had come to his home last night after her husband slipped out of the house using business as an excuse. She had wanted some of his time, only to discover he wasn't home. Paula, on the other hand, had sent a message mentioning her time with him and how her body was still feeling the ropes and his touch. Tanya wanted a set time they would meet up again. All of these women were vying for his time and attention not realizing what was coming their way, he thought.

After reading their messages he deleted them before calling up SK to see what he wanted. The phone rang a few times before he picked up.

"What's good, my dude? Them broads holding you hostage?" SK asked soon as he picked up.

"Nah. I just got up when I heard my

phone ringing."

"You sick or dying?" SK asked being partially funny knowing Jaelen was always up early.

"Late night, fool. I was securing the bag with the real number one," he said, now giving Laila the Number One code name instead of Tanya.

"Who's that?"

"You already know that one that was playing hard to get," he said, making him aware of who he was with.

"Mont said you was onto something?"

"Yeah, when we meet up, I'll put y'all onto it. We good though, trust me. If this goes right, we can retire with close to a half a hundred." Hearing Jaelen say this, SK already figured Laila and her husband must have more than the couple thousand they discovered at the first glance.

"Say no more. We'll be over later so we can really put this together. Shit, we can get it done now if you're ready," SK said, wondering to himself why they would wait when everything had come together as they planned, but sooner than expected.

"Patience, my friend, patience."

SK, hearing Jaelen's tone, which didn't sound confident as it usually did, was concern-ed.

"I hope you didn't lose control over your situation when you were with baby girl."

Jaelen's face turned up. He didn't want his friends to think he was weak in any way. "You of all people know I have this under control. Nothing is going to stop me from getting what I want, or reaching our end game, and that's walking away from all of this on top," he said. "You just focus on what your part is in all of this." He hung up, slightly pissed at what SK had said and at himself for having twisted thoughts and emotions that lingered from last night and the dream he had awoken from.

He scrolled to the next number he had to call: Monty's. A part of him was dreading it because if both of his associates thought he was slipping in any way, hindering this multimillion dollar deceptive heist, they could consider removing him. Otherwise it could backfire, exposing who they were, especially since the people they'd gotten thus far never expected them even til this day.

He tapped the phone, calling up Monty. He wanted to hear what he had to say, since he had called a few times. Monty picked up on the second ring.

"Yo, what's going on with you over there? Baby doll got you cuffed to the bed or something?" Monty said. Jaelen gave a light laugh wishing he and Laila would have explored the cuff thing. Maybe next time.

"I'm good. I had a late night making sure we are all on the same page."

"So, what you find out on the computer?"

"It's all there. I'll fill you and SK in play by play, plus I'll show you what I retrieved. He's smart but we always think ahead, making us smarter than him."

"I also came across something with the women. Something that looks suspect."

"What is it?" Jaelen asked, now fully awake in game mode.

"Plane tickets purchased by two of the women. One flying out to Aspen, Colorado. The other flying to Juno,

Alaska."

"Those are two winter destinations for vacation. You're overthinking it," Jaelen res-ponded.

"They're both one-way flights on the exact same day."

Hearing this now piqued his interest, wondering which ladies it was and what they were up to, if anything at all.

"Which two is it?"

"The grocer and the dealer," he resp-onded referring to Danna, whose husband owned the chain of stores, and Paula, whose fiancé was the car dealer.

"I'll check baby doll's activity to see if she has a flight around that date too."

"How far out are their flights?"

"Two weeks from today," he said, hearing Jaelen let out a stressed breath trying to process how he was going to pull this back together and take control of this situation.

"Don't worry, I'll handle it and give them a reason to stick around, without letting them know I know their plans."

"In the meantime, I'll continue to keep watch, securing my end."

Jaelen hung up only to send each of

the women—Danna, Paula, and Tanya—a message. He was arranging time with each of them, starting with Danna, then Paula and Tanya.

He messaged each of the women, piquing their curiosity with his intimate texts as if he was yearning to be in their presence, each of them falling into the image of his words of how he wanted to do things to them and with them. Little did they know he had tens of millions on the line that made every pass at them worth it.

FOUR

12:34 p.m.

Jaelen met up with Danna at Gilligan's Sports Bar & Grill, for lunch. He figured this was on the edge of the city far from his place and hers. He saw her exiting her car looking amazing in her black jeans, with brown suede D&G and her hair down displaying her silky hair, enhancing her natural Asian beauty. He exited the truck wearing Gucci sneakers with YSL navy blue jeans flowing with his lightweight black leather jacket by Gucci. He made his way over to her unnoticed until he spoke.

"Angels do exist." She turned hearing his voicing lighting up with a smile that was warm and welcoming. Her eyes also smiled, feeling good about being in his presence.

"Thank you. That's nice of you to say, but being here with you doesn't make me an angel. At least my husband wouldn't think so," she said, making him rethink his statement. He smiled as he processed his own words.

"Danna, your husband is not here with you for a reason, because you want to be with me and share my space," he said, pulling her close and placing a kiss to her lips. She didn't resist welcoming him, allowing her to flash back to the shower that took her mind, heart, and body by storm. A part of her wanted to know how this lunch date was going to end. "Now let's go eat, I'm starving," he said, leading the way.

Once inside they ordered their food and drinks. They had found their way into the corner booth, giving them the privacy he needed to have all of her attention. He kept it light, ordering wine but keeping it to one glass, not wanting to be drunk. He needed to have all of his focus. As for Danna, she was on her third glass of wine halfway through her meal.

"Danna, I brought you here today because I want to expand our scope of intimate play. I want to travel with you to different places and have erotic moments around the globe, being adventurous, yet keeping what we have interesting at all times." Hearing his words only turned her on even more, making her want to go anywhere with him as long as she got the best part of each trip, which was him and his tight body.

"Mmmh, that sounds good. Anything with you included will be good."

He set the trap for her, seeing if she was willing. Now he was going to lure her in further.

"Name a place you've never been, and we'll start from there," he said, looking on at her as she was sipping her wine to chase down the lamb she had ordered.

"Niagara Falls. I can see the two of us getting as close as we possibly can to the falls allowing the roaring waters crashing down to vibrate our bodies as we get lost in one another's embrace feeling the mist racing over us."

The images he had as she was describing it were vivid, making him actually want to try it.

"How about the thirty-first of this month, just me and you?" he asked, knowing that's the date of her flight to Aspen. She smiled taking a bite of her lamb looking on at him processing her answer. He could see this in her eyes, so he followed up. "Unless you have plans already for that day?"

"I'll go anywhere, any day with you, as long as I figure out how to get away from my husband without him becoming suspicious," she responded. Her words brought some calm to him since she didn't avoid that date.

"Good. Now that we have that out of the way, after we leave here, I want to take you to this adult toy store, so we can travel with a little fun."

Her mind raced thinking about the toy store, another first for her since her husband didn't use them and she didn't own any of her own. The closest she'd come to a toy was watching on television.

"Ooooh, you're really trying to turn me into a bad girl. You want to spank me across this table, tie me up in the dark?" she said, being funny yet licking her lips before sipping the remainder of her wine. He was enjoying her humor, but at the same time he was ready to further secure things with her so he could head to his next date with Paula.

"We're down here. It's time to play," he said, getting up from the table making his way over to her, assisting her from the booth. She was feeling the buzz from the glasses of wine. It was also turning her on knowing they were about to be bad in the most sexual adult way.

He left six $20 bills for the food and tip before exiting with her. He took her keys and placed them in his pocket since she had had a little too much to drink, making her unable to drive.

He helped her into the truck before getting in himself and driving roughly a mile down the road where the adult toy store was off the highway. The adult toy was off the highway. The adult toy store had a strip club in one half of the building, giving its customers the full experience of a one-stop shop. As soon as they entered, they were greeted by two females standing tall in their six-inch pumps, with red and black lingerie, tassels, and whips in hand looking the part of dominants.

"Welcome to This Is How We Play adult toy store and strip club. If there's anything we can help you with, please don't be afraid to ask," they said, smiling and swaying their hips looking on at Danna as if she was their next meal. They too appreciated her Asian beauty.

"I know what I'm looking for," Jaelen said walking past the ladies holding onto Danna's hand and leading the way.

Danna's looked on at the sex wheel with cuffs and the makeshift nurses' station with employees in full costume demonstrating with the toys. Her mind was racing seeing all of this, along with the variety of dildos, some looking real and flesh-like, leather ropes, anal balls and tasers, which really had her confused wondering why someone would want to be stunned for sexual purposes.

"I want you to have an open mind. Even if you're scared to try certain things, understand fear can sometimes induce pleasure as your adrenaline is spiked."

Hearing him speaking about being in fear was making her timid about what was to come, but the level of curiosity had her interest.

"Stand right here while I pick out a few things. If you see something you like or think of something, let me know," he said, vanishing into the store. He went off purchasing multiple toys knowing he was going to have to get into her heart and mind through her body. He came back with a bag of toys he had just bought. "You ready to let me take you to this new place of passion?"

"I hope so," she responded, taking his hand. "Are you going to let me tie you up and do bad things to your body that will make my body feel good?" she said, making him laugh. He led the way to the back of the store where they had pleasure showrooms that they designed for people's homes. Jaelen, taking advantage of the crowed store, led her into the mirrored pleasure showroom and shut the door. There were floor to ceiling mirrors with metal mounts, leather seating, and red lighting for setting the mood for passion. He knew he was not going to have long, so he had to move fast. He secured the door, locking it. This sent slight fear into Danna, about being in a public place, getting caught, and her husband finding out.

"What are you doing?" she asked.

"We're going to get lost in each other's presence," he said, closing in on her and placing a kiss to her lips. "Take your clothes off, leave your heels on." He took his shirt off exposing his glistening cut frame she remembered from the shower. His pants came off just as she stood in the nude only wearing her heels as he requested. "Put your hands on the mirror." She obliged, glancing over at him taking a few items from the bag, including a life-like dildo that was vibrating. Seeing this was turning her on, knowing he was going to use it on her. He also had oil in one hand along with something else she couldn't make out right away. He squeezed the oil down her back allowing it to flow over her bottom into the crease of her ass. "Without pain we would never know what pleasure is," he said, coming up behind her and placing his thickness and length up against her bottom and pushing her back side, creating pressure on her asshole.

"Aaaaah, I never did this," she let out, removing her left hand from the mirror and placing it on his thickness as if to halt it.

"Put your hand back on the mirror. I'll take care of your every desire first," he said, pressing into her and entering her body. She tensed up, letting out a moan of pain and pleasure. He could see it in her eyes through the mirror that she now liked the feeling in her body. The fear she had prior was also turning her on. He introduced the vibrating dildo to her V, creating an instant sensation of pleasure as he started stroking her from behind while moving the vibrator in and out of her body.

"Ooooooh my, ooooooh my, oooooh, mmmmmmh." She was moaning trying to process what was taking place with her body, having two things inside of her giving her pain and pleasure all at the same time. She felt this buildup of orgasms wanting to be released, and her heart was racing as she was looking over by the door wondering if customers or employees heard her moans. "Ooooooh my, mmmmmmh." Her head went back and forth in between looking down at the vibrator going in and out of her body. Her heart and mind were racing feeling this surging of pleasure taking over her body. Then it happened: he raised the purple taser that was set on low and pressed it against her butt cheek, squeezing it. The sound of it going off scared her more than the actual stinging she felt. This turned her on even more. "Aaaaah, ooooh, that was scary good, mmmmmmh," she let out.

Their moment of play came to a halt when an employee started knocking on the door.

"Excuse me, you can't be in there with this door locked! It's against our rules and the law!" a female voice came through the door. Danna's fears were confirmed: she was busted, and her husband would find out. Jaelen ignored the employee, turned on even more, and continued on stroking deep into Danna's body while moving the vibrator even faster, making her fears of getting caught shift to pleasure as she started to release multiple orgasms. He too felt himself exploding into her body as he was slamming harder, deeper, and faster before coming to a slow. Her face was close to the mirror breathing heavily, steaming it up. He removed himself and the vibrator from her body, before getting dressed. She still remained with her hands on the mirror as her body was releasing, feeling open from what he'd just done to her. Her eyes became glassy knowing what was taking place was so wrong yet so good. She finally turned to him ignoring the knocking on the door from the employee. "Mmmmmh, ooooh my. My body is in love with your touch," she let out, finally moving from her position and getting her clothes on. "I can't believe the things you have me doing, or how I feel when you're done," she said, shaking her head and now fully dressed, fixing herself and preparing to exit.

"Too bad we got interrupted, or I would have shown you a few more things. That will have to wait until the thirty-first," he said, throwing that out there again to see what her response was.

"I look forward to that day and more," she responded as he opened the door. The female employee looked on at the two of them as they passed by her as if she didn't exist. Jaelen and Danna both felt good as they left the adult toy store feeling rediscovered.

FIVE

2:36 p.m.

Jaelen met up with Paula at the Harrisburg East Mall after he raced home, showered again, and changed his clothes and his fragrance to make himself fresh for his date with her. He needed to know if the thirty-first of this month meant anything to her other than her flight to Juno, Alaska. A part of him wanted it to be pure coincidence, but the thinking and paranoid side of him knew something was not right with this. He just needed to get behind it all.

Jaelen decided to meet Paula by Macy's front entrance since that was where he would be taking her shopping. She came up looking good in her black jeans, black six-inch pumps that enhanced her already filled out curves of perfection. The pink Givenchy top flowed over her perky breasts, making her lightly glossed pink lips stand out more the closer she stepped in his direction. Her eyes glowed just as much as her smile, making him feel good about seeing her, and at the same time making him want her right now, right there. She was also taking in his good looks with this Giorgio Armani loafers flowing with the denim jeans, with the black Kenneth Cole cotton button-up shirt that fit his body snuggly, displaying his muscles. The diamond-encrusted Frank Muller Double Mystery Collection also stood out, making him look even more refined and handsome in her eyes.

"You look like a distinguished gentleman, Jaelen," she said, eyeing him up and down as she placed her hand on his bicep, feeling it through his fitted shirt. He removed her hand and placed a kiss to it.

"You also look amazing. Standing out in a crowd is easy for you to do, I guess, being as sexy as you are with that Custom Fit Body," he said, taking the credit.

"Your gym is to thank for more than fitness," she said, reflecting back to him tying her up with the jump ropes. The feeling her body experienced had left an emotional and mental imprint on her that would last a lifetime.

He took her hand and led the way into the store as he began to speak, wanting to feel her out.

"I was thinking about you all day after our time at the gym. I was wanting more of you and your time. But I want it to be special, like me taking you somewhere we can let go and be ourselves."

Her mind followed his every word, wanting to be set free in his world of passion and pleasure. "What do you have in mind?"

"Miami, where we can party, play on

the beach, and be sexy at the same time while enjoying each other's space."

"Mmmh, I can feel the warmth of the sand on my body and feet just thinking about it. I can't wait," she said.

"I checked and already made reservations for the thirty-first of this month since I figured you would be willing to spend time with me," he said, stopping to look at her and checking her demeanor to see if it shifted in any way. She brought her hand up to his chest and caressed it, looking into his eyes and raising up on her toes placing a kiss to his lips as her french manicured nails softly caressed his neck stimulating him with her soft touch. Then she halted, pulling back from the kiss.

"The way you made me feel at the gym, and how much I wanted more of you from that moment, I can't think of a better place to be or go as long as I'm getting all of you," she responded with lust in her eyes. She was turned on, wanting him right now. He could see this in her eyes. Now that he had his answers from both women, he had to figure out if they both were going to cancel their previous engagements with their trips on the same date. If so, he was going to be in a bind having to appease both of these women with the trips he had promised them. As these thoughts were entering his mind, Paula's hand started roaming over his body, getting his attention.

"Let's focus before we have customers thinking they can get a free show," he said, taking her hand and leading the way. "Now I want you to grab a few things you think will look sexy in Miami. I'll stand over here because I want you to surprise me with all of your sexy attire."

"What if I need your help in the dressing room?" she said, giving him this naughty girl look. A smile formed on his face assessing the area where the dressing room was. His creative genius was kicking in. At the same time thoughts of the millions he was going to walk away with stimulated his thoughts even more. She saw that he was in thought, so she added, "Surprise me as you just said." She smiled, turning and walking away, allowing him to take in her curvaceous body and nice ass that was strutting away bouncing with each step. She knew he was looking, because he liked to tease as much as he also teased her. He folded his arms looking around the store processing his next move.

He watched her shopping before she vanished into the dressing room. Jaelen didn't budge; he stood there wanting her to want him even more. At the same time, she was inside of the dressing room trying on her things and glancing over at the door through the mirror wall looking for him to enter. Her thoughts drifted to what she wanted done to her body if and when he entered.

A few minutes passed by, and she

peeked out of the dressing room to see if he was still standing with his arms folded. Nothing, he was gone. Where was he? She wondered. At the same time her cell phone sounded off with a message alert. She stepped back into the dressing room to check her phone seeing who was messaging her. It came up anonymous, but the content gave her an idea of who it was.

"Who's that?" a voice came from above her head. It jolted her in fear, startled by Jaelen's voice coming from the top side of the other dressing room looking down on her. She deleted the text in the process of slipping her phone back into her tight jean back pocket.

"My fiancé wondering why I didn't stop by the car lot before going shopping," she responded. Jaelen looked on at her knowing she was hiding something. He would have to figure out what it was, in case it hindered his multi-million-dollar plans.

A part of him didn't even wanting to be sexual with her, but something came to mind as he stepped down and made his way around to the dressing room she was in.

He entered with silk scarfs. It didn't register to her what he was about to do. She figured they looked nice with her clothing.

"Come over here." She took a step close to him, and he grabbed a silk scarf and placed it around her neck. Then he allowed the other to drape over her shoulder, flowing over her powder-blue bra and panty set. He took the long scarf and guided it into her panties over her pearl, only to pull it slightly out the back side of her panties. Then he took his free hand around to the back of her neck and wrapped a scarf around her neck, twirling it to constrict around her neck. Her eyes widened as fear kicked in. "Keep your eyes on me," he said, tightening the scarf. "Do I have your best interest?" he asked, eyeing her yet tightening his grip on the scarf while taking his other hand and reaching around her to take hold of the other scarf hanging out of the bottom of her panties. She could feel a light caressing of the silk scarf over her pearl, stimulating her body at the same time fear was streaming through her body as he was constricting the other scarf around her neck.

"Yes, it's getting tight," she responded. He pulled the scarf in her panties, allowing it to move a foot, sending pleasure through her body yet confusing her mind as fear was racing through her mind and body just as this wave of pleasure. "Aaaah, aaaah, what's happening?" she asked, never before feeling good about being confused. He closed in and placed his lips against hers, squeezing the scarf while pulling the other scarf all the way out, sliding over her pearl and making her moan. "Aaaaah, aaaaah, mmmmh, stop, stop, mmmmmmh." He loosened his grip enough for her to enjoy the pleasure of the scarf down low being removed. She gasped for air, still having fear in her eyes. Now his free hand went down over her belly into her panties. H slid his thick fingers over her pearl, at the same time constricting the scarf once more while guiding her body to the wall. She could feel his finger entering into her body, stirring up pleasure and making her heart thump in pleasure as butterflies were soaring through her. The scarf tightened even more, partially because he was angered by the feeling of betrayal. This was one of the reasons he didn't believe in love. He was torn at a young age and had never fully returned from that pain. He was looking into her eyes seeing the fear coupled with euphoria as her body was streaming with orgasms racing over his fingers. "Aaaah, ooooh, nooo, ooooh, noooo, mmmmmmh stop, stop, mmmh," she said in fear, feeling herself losing breath. She could also feel her heart beating in her neck as he constricted the scarf more. Right then he released and removed the scarf, and at the same time she let out an orgasmic moan just as her body shook with a wave of pleasure. "Aaaaaah, mmmmh, mmmh, okay, okay, okay," she let out as if she was ready to tell him who really was messaging her. He became attentive seeing this. Suddenly she regained herself and pulled it all together. "I want more of this, but I really have to go right now. My fiancé will be either calling or looking for me soon. He tries to track my phone," she said, pulling herself together and getting her clothes on. Seeing this heightened his level of acuity, knowing he was going to have to think ahead, and fast.

"I hope you have all of this figured out before we leave on the thirty-first, because I wouldn't want him popping up on us on the beach," Jaelen said.

"I won't allow anything to ruin what we have planned on the thirty-first," she said, leaning in and placing a kiss on his lips before rubbing his chest. "I want all that you've been hiding from me." Her hand lowered to his manhood, tapping the outside of his pants before exiting the dressing room.

He followed, paying for her clothes before kissing her goodbye. He didn't feel like he had her under control as he did Danna. It just didn't feel right. He didn't like this feeling one bit, especially with him always being the preeminent one.

SIX

3:52 p.m.

Jaelen was at his place waiting for SK and Monty to show up so they could go over the business and check into a few things, as well as address the thirty-first which was bothering him. As he was waiting, he scrolled his web page checking out new clients for his gym along with postings clients had made giving him good reviews. He noticed Laura and Candice; Laila's friends also had given him good reviews. They also mentioned how they couldn't wait until the next class.

Shifting his focus from the page, he saw an incoming text from Laila. He sat back on the couch and accessed the message. It read:

"Last night was so good. Thought I was dreaming. Woke up late. L.O.L."

He laughed reading the text knowing

he too felt the same way but didn't want to just throw it out there. "You can have what you want if you ask for it."

He sent the message wanting to tweak her mind yet make her ask him to come over again. He wanted to have her again, but this time it wouldn't be for the money: it would be to get inside of her heart, mind, and body. She would never know it was him or his associates that wiped their bank accounts clean because nothing would ever point back to them. He would also keep his day-to-day business operations running, filtering the money through other business ventures.

He could have her and the life he was partially thinking of with her. He didn't think of love when it came to her; he somehow viewed her as his equal, but never allow her to be aware of this.

"I get what I want. I don't need to ask if what I want desires the same." Her words were true yet keeping him on his feet, keeping this back-and-forth word play interesting.

"How much of what you like can you resist when it's right before you?" He sent the text, changing up the direction.

She received the text and read it,

flashing back to how erotic last night was, from the workout session, to the tub, into the bedroom, and throughout the night until he left. She didn't want him to leave. It was his choice. How could he be so close and she not have a night like that again, she gave a light laugh, smiling inside and out not wanting to respond and give him the answer she knew he wanted. She placed her phone down wanting to have the upper hand.

Jaelen was looking on at his phone awaiting her response. Nothing. Long minutes passed by before he too placed his phone down not wanting to give in to her so easily. He focused back on the web page, checking his reviews and comments. Strange as it was, he came across a comment Laila had posted two days after she joined the gym: "C.B.F. is the gym for me. The trainer welcomes you into his space making each class feel one-on-one. He really gets the woman's body and how to get fit."

Jaelen, reading this, starting smiling, feeling as if she may be the balance he was looking for, especially if she broke it off with her husband. He reached over preparing to grab his cell phone to send Laila a message, when a message from her came through.

"You win."

Two words that made him feel closer to her yet preeminent. He responded playing dumbfounded, "The prize (You?)"

Laila held the cell phone close to her heart as if it was him she was hugging, making her feel the comfort. "My pace @ UR place," she responded.

He read the text suggesting her pace, meaning she wanted to be in control. He gave it some thought, wanting to lure her in, knowing the control would be all his. "I'll claim my prize @ 8 sharp," he sent.

She read it smiling that he was using the relation of the prize factor, which allowed her to know how he felt since she posed the question to him, of what was more important to him, the prize or the reward.

She got herself together preparing to entertain and be entertained for the night.

Jaelen, on the other hand, was making his way over to the door to answer the bell that had just sounded off. He looked through the peephole and saw his associates, Monty and SK.

"Yo, what's good with y'all?" he said,

welcoming them into this condo.

"We focused on getting these M's," SK said, giving Jaelen a dap.

"Wait until you see this shit," Monty said, shaking Jaelen's hand.

"Take a seat, I got beers coming y'all's way in a second," he said, heading into the kitchen and taking three Molson XXX beers from the freezer before coming back out over to the living room area. "Here y'all go right here. So what you got, Monty?"

"First fill us in on that sexy-ass Laila you was with last night," SK said. "I know that thing's special."

Jaelen had to check himself before reacting or responding in a manner that would alarm his associates, since he was starting to like her in a way he shouldn't, going against their business code.

"She got gifts, but that's not what I was really there for," he said, shifting it away from their intimate time only to focus on the money aspect of it. "Her husband's little mistress's name, Farah Cantrelle, was the password to getting into this computer. They have seventeen million in multiple accounts."

"Goddamn it, man," SK let out before drinking some of his beer. "I am partying in Brazil after this. I can see it now: models and bottles, baby." SK was getting hyped.

"No one is going anywhere," Monty said. "That's not how we handle business. We stay in place as if we know nothing or as if it never happened." He paused, drinking some of his beer before adding, "Jaelen, you got at those other two?" he asked, referring to Danna and Paula.

"Danna seemed like she wasn't

aware of her prior arrangements. She was all for leaving town that day. As for Paula, she had something else going on in her life I couldn't figure out, plus I crept up on her receiving a call or text. When I made my presence known, she was alarmed."

"I'll tie that bitch up if she fucks this up," SK blurted.

"SK, you know we don't use those tactics. We use the greatest weapon there is, our brains, and right now you seem to be losing yours with all of this partying you want to do along with tying people up," Jaelen said.

"This is the biggest drop we've ever come across all at once. Of course, I'm approaching this with another side," SK responded. Both Jaelen and Monty continued on with the conversations.

"I did a little further research on our ladies you met up with earlier. Their flights are on the same day with no return back here; however, I noticed both of them on the following day of their arrivals at their destination also have flights to LAX. Here's where it gets good: they each get on the same flight to Dubai."

Hearing Monty say this, SK and Jaelen both became fully alert that something just wasn't right.

"Them bitches have something up their sleeves, and you still want to take the 'let me use my brain' approach?" SK said, thinking about the tens of millions on the line. It didn't work if these women were not in play. Unless they avoided Danna's and Paula's spouse's accounts and focused on Tanya and Laila, which combined was close to thirty million. Still more than they'd schemed before.

"We make our move within the next

few days. We can't give any of them enough time to be ahead of us, especially after today with me asking the two of them to go on a trip with me. If they're getting on that flight together, it means they're communicating with one another and they each know that I asked them to come with me on the thirty-first, so they're either going to wait on that day or try to move it up. Either way we move in a few days. No later than Tuesday," he said, knowing today was Saturday. That would give him and his team time to access all accounts simultaneously and send the money overseas, where it would be bounced around to multiple accounts before reaching the Bahamian account they had in a bogus name.

"I'll program my computer to keep an alert on anything that pops up with them as far as changes to their flights, or credit card activity."

"I can't double back on them, trying to lure them in or get more info, because it would be obvious that I figured them out," Jaelen said.

"Like you said, you asked both of them out on the date they're flying out. It's going to spook them a little. We just have to keep a close eye and see how much," Monty said. SK drank the remainder of his ice-cold beer wanting to move now, the best way he knew how, but he was following his team. So he didn't say anything.

"All right, fellas, while you two keep tabs on them, I'm about to stay close to baby doll. I'm having her over tonight for a little replay," Jaelen said, standing and preparing to walk his associates out.

"Don't lose focus, fool," SK said, getting up making his way to the door. "Remember what I told you: we're good at what we do, but there's no creature more deceptive than a female."

"No female has outsmarted us yet. Last I checked, we're winning," Jaelen said. "Monty, show him the numbers. Men lie, women lie, my back account don't." He laughed at his own words, tilting his beer back as his friends made their way out of the condo. As soon as the door shut, he snapped. "Son of a bitch!" he let out, realizing he had allowed these two women to conjure up whatever it was they were doing without him being up on it. He was not feeling in control. In fact, he was feeling as if these two had slipped through his grasp. Now he would have to figure out what would bring them back under his control. Right now, he had to get things in order for his guest tonight. For once, he was going to escape this feeling he was having, into her place of passion.

SEVEN

7:58 p.m.

Jaelen checked his watch in between looking up at the door awaiting Laila's arrival. He had everything laid out: a little drink, crushed ice on the side, some passion fruits—strawberries and grapes—with a heated bowl of white chocolate along with some Hershey's dark chocolate. He also had wine to accompany the fruit-and-chocolate foreplay. The bed had been arranged with white satin sheets, plush pillows, and red candles leading from the living room to the bedroom. If SK and Monty could see this, they would abort the mission or go ahead and get everything done right now knowing their associate had slipped into a place where they didn't recognize him. He even had a dozen roses sent to his place. He took six of the roses and spread them around the table with the chocolate, fruits, and wines, completing the intimate look. The rest of the roses he plucked, and laid rose petals leading from the front door to the table of passion.

He checked his watch and saw it was 7:59 p.m. His eyes glanced over to his phone and saw it hadn't sounded off, no incoming calls. He took another look around the condo making sure everything was in place. He took a grape from the silver tray and ate it as he walked over by the door looking out of the peephole. Nothing. He turned, walking away, and then it happened: a knock across the door. He couldn't deceive himself; he lit up smiling feeling good inside and out, especially when he glanced through the peephole seeing it was her. He took a step back taking a calm breath preparing to take control. He opened the door, and she too lit with a smile seeing him in these all-black Armani two-piece silk pajamas set with slippers boasting his initials in gold lettering matching the gold lettering on his pajama top.

He too was taking in her beauty standing there in an all-white quarter-length fur coat, her hair looking wet pulled back, makeup done just right, eyes glowing, her red lipstick popping off of the white coat she opened, exposing her sexy body that was filling out a red negligee. His excitement was ready to leap out of him, but he was holding it together realizing the art of her goddess-like body had officially lured him all of the way in. The flowing coat flowing down over her silky smooth tanned legs that seamlessly slid into the six-inch pumps she was wearing added to her exotic look.

"You really came to play looking the part of a goddess," he said, stepping to the side allowing her to pass by. She entered, only to halt and place a kiss on his lips before walking and taking in all of the arrangements.

"You're a thoughtful gentleman, I see," she said, looking down at the rose petals leading over to the table of passion, fruits, and chocolates. "You have a lot planned. I have a lot for you to resist," she let out, looking over her shoulders at him before he shut the door. She made her way over to the table, taking a strawberry and biting into it.

"You didn't ask for that," he said, walking over to her.

"I'm hungry," she said, being smart, her way of taking control.

"Sometimes we have to learn to resist our cravings," he said, taking the remaining piece of strawberry from her grasp and placing it on the table. "Stand right there. Allow me to enjoy feeding your every desire," he said, taking a strawberry and dipping it into the hot melted chocolate before bringing it back around to her. She thought he was going to feed it to her until he lowered to one knee and placed the hot chocolate up against her inner thigh. She squirmed from the chair, looking down at him closing in on her place of intimacy while painting her inner thigh with the chocolate. His tongue followed, cleaning up the chocolate streak. He closed in on her negligee and lifted it, allowing his fingertips to caress the lips of her place of passion before sliding the strawberry into her negligee and pressing it up against her pearl. Her eyes closed feeling her heart fluttering at this touch. "Don't move, I need it to be held in place," he directed, wanting the strawberry to tease her body along with his kisses that were placed around her V taunting her. She could feel the strawberry sliding the more she was being turned on from his touch, her fluids lubricating and making it slide. As it was moving, she was also being turned on by it. Her mouth was open with sexual sighs knowing how much she wanted his tongue on her body, because thoughts of how it was last night made her melt inside, wanting him but knowing she had to resist it. He reached for another strawberry, dipping it into the hot white chocolate and placing it to her other leg, then allowing his tongue to trail up to her V. He reached his hand under her, placing his finger on her bottom hole and creating pressure as he placed the strawberry into her negligee, adding more pressure on her pearl. "Resist that good feeling," he said as she looked down at him trying to hold her position and resist this good feeling he was imposing on her body. He reached for another strawberry, dipped it into the dark chocolate, and put it into her V. She let out a moan.

"Ooooh no, mmmmmmh." He was doing things to her she'd never imagined. Then he took the other two strawberries inside her negligee and placed them into her V as well, creating a light stimulating pressure. That was just the beginning.

"Hold them in place while resisting as much of what's to come as you can," he said, keeping her negligee to the side as his fingers and tongue entered into play. He cornered her pearl between his fingertips and tongue, while his other hand went back to placing pressure on her bottom.

"Ooooooh, God nooo, I can't, I can't, mmmmmmh, mmmmmmh," she moaned, unable to hold back the good feeling that was taking over her body as she was trying to hold the strawberries in and hold back the wave of pleasure he was sending into her body. His tongue

137

and fingers were moving fast, making her legs shake. Her V was constricting, holding onto the strawberries, and her moans were intensifying as the orgasmic buildup was reaching its peak of eruption wanting to be released. "You win, mmmmmmh, mmmmmmh, mmmmmmh, ooooh God, oooooooh God," she let out, feeling the fluids flowing through her body at a pulsating rate, making her heart flutter. Her mind raced and her body shook under the spell of his tongue and fingers. Her hands were now on his head holding him in place as she was embracing the uncontrollable feeling and the power of pleasure taking her by storm. "Okay, okay, okay, mmmmmmh, mmmmmmh," she let out, no longer able to hold the strawberries in while her body was releasing with great pleasure. Her hips moved, gyrating and feeling his finger on her bottom. He came to halt and stood as he reached down and slid his fingers into her negligee, removing each of the strawberries only to bring them up and place them to her lips.

"Now you can eat," he said, also taking one and placing it to his lips before they each took one and ate it. "Take a seat. That was the introduction to what's to come tonight," he said. She obliged gladly, feeling her sensitive body still reacting to his tongue and fingers as if they were still in place. He poured glasses of wine for the two of them before they continued on with conversation that stimulated their hearts, minds, and bodies. "That's twice in one day you said I win," he reminded her.

"Now that doesn't count. I was caught up in the moment," she responded, sipping her wine.

"You said what you meant. If you didn't mean to say it, or if you weren't thinking or feeling that way, it wouldn't have come out. Don't worry, it feels good to let go and allow someone else to be in control of your body, taking you to that place of unexpected desire and passion," he said, taking some grapes and feeding them to her. His finger was close to her lips, and she leaned in biting down on his index finger. Alarmed by her action, he looked into her eyes turned on by this. She could see he liked a little pain with his play.

"My turn to see how much you can resist," she said, taking his hand and holding onto it while kissing the top of his hand before slipping his fingers across her lips. She was still looking into his eyes as she bit down lightly and saw it was turning him on. She placed his hand on her breast as she leaned in for the kiss, he closed his eyes until he felt her bite down on his lips, sending this pain and pleasure through him. This lip biting led to her kisses trailing to his neck as her free hand found his love stick and caressed it to length. She bit into his neck, feeling his breath exhaling and enjoying the torment of pain and pleasure. She opened his button-up pajamas top, displaying his cut chest, and continued caressing him through his clothing as her lips found his chest and nipple and bit down. Another heated breath escaped his mouth. Her hand now went into his pajamas, feeling the veins pulsating in his length and thickness. Her touch was soft yet stimulating to him. She pulled his length from his pajamas and went down kissing the top before kissing the side as she stroked him with soft hands, her free hand caressing his cut abs before her manicured nails pressed deep into them. At the same time her lips parted, taking him into her mouth briefly and teasing him as he felt the warmth and wetness of her mouth.

"Damn, this feels good," he let out as her nails continued pressing into his flesh, followed by her lips gliding up and down on him assisted by her soft hand going up and down creating pleasure making him feel like he was ready to bust. Then he was jolted with pain as she removed her mouth and bit down lightly on the side of his manhood. Most men would halt this process, figuring the woman doesn't know what she's doing down there. However, he didn't feel this way. He was actually inviting more of this pain and pleasure. Her hand speed picked up, creating even more sensation and allowing him to get closer and closer to his release. His hips moved lightly, thrusting into her grasp and feeling the buildup in his body wanting to be released. It was getting closer and closer. Now her lips found him once more, bringing him even closer to his powerful eruption that was taking over, ready to be freed. Her nails pressed down hard on his abs as she too could feel him about to cum with the veins in his thickness pulsating more the faster she went. Then she stopped. She removed her nails, mouth, and hand from him. He opened his eyes, breathing heavily and wanting her to finish. "It was right there," he was thinking and feeling. "No, no, no. Why'd you stop?" he asked, breathing heavily and fully erect at the edge of eruption. Her eyes locked on him.

"Resist the urge to feel completion," she said, coming close to his length and thickness and breathing on it with her eyes still locked on him. He wanted and needed her to finish. He had never had this happen. Most women would savor every bit of him. He was right there at the peak, just a few more pumps with her lips and touch. She pressed her nails into his thighs, inflicting pain that triggered pleasure followed by the closeness of her mouth to his thickness. Then her lips touched the side of it.

"Oh shit, damn, damn, damn, you got me," he let out, closing his eyes having never had this reaction to a female's touch, the art of her control taking him by surprise. "How did she do this?" he was thinking, yet loving how his body was reacting to all of the pain-induced pleasure. She came up to his side allowing her nails to follow up to his chest.

Then she leaned in and whispered, "I WIN." She nibbled on his ear before caressing his chest in a sensual manner. His eyes were still closed enjoying this moment. For once he didn't mind how it felt to give up a little control.

Moments later after he regained himself, he turned to her and placed a kiss on her lips that was now full of passion.

"It's going to be a long night of this back and forth thing, but I'm looking forward to claiming my prize before it's all said and done," he said, taking his hand

and placing it over her heart. This caught her off guard. She didn't know how to react. In this moment her heart felt something for him too. This feeling of wanting him became more than sex. She wanted to share his space, the adventure and the excitement he'd brought into her life. The only thing was, how would this play out with her husband?

Jaelen also realized his actions of placing his hand over her heart meant he was willing to venture into a place he had long turned his back on. A place he stopped believing in because of heartbreak. However, for her he could see something that would make this different and worth the while. He could actually find that balance, or in other words, he could find love. If so, this would change the dynamic of his life and lifestyle, including the cons that had made him so successful. But what good is money and success if it can't be shared with someone worth making memories with, he was thinking as their lips found one another caught in this sexually charged emotional moment.

EIGHT

9:42 a.m.

The next morning Jaelen was jolted from his sleep when a loud banging came across his condo door followed by his cell phone ringing. He sat up quickly, looking to the other side of the bed where Laila's body once lay snuggled next to his. She had left in the middle of the night smiling and enjoying their erotic session that was way more intense than the first. They each discovered a lot more about one another on a personal level, piquing each of their interest. He turned back to his still ringing cell phone seeing that it was SK calling. Seeing this number and hearing someone banging on his door, a bad vibe came to him.

"Talk to me," Jaelen said, answering the phone.

"They got us! Get the fuck up outta bed and answer the door!" SK said.

Hearing what he said jolted Jaelen even more.

"Who got us?" he asked, rushing to the front door and opening it only to see SK and Monty looking pissed. He hung the phone up and stepped to the side to allow them in.

"They took the muthafucking money," SK snapped. "I knew I should have approached this shit different."

"Calm down, we still have the other paper to chase," Jaelen said, looking at SK then Monty, who was shaking his head.

"We don't have anything to chase. I programmed the shit last night to start draining all of the accounts, to go through our usual process. Then I checked this morning only to discover someone piggybacked on our transaction, adding more money. To top it off they wiped all of our accounts, using our same method and sending our money to their overseas accounts that somehow vanished once I attempted to trace them." Hearing Monty speaking made Jaelen's ear turn deaf as his body became numb in pain of losing the absolute power and control he thought he had.

"So you're telling me we're broke?" Jaelen snapped.

"Them bitches got us! I knew something wasn't right!" SK blurted out, revealing his nickel-plated 10mm Colt for the first time. "I'm going to blow their fucking head off for this."

"That's not how we're going to handle this. You do that, we go to jail. We know where they're going; we follow them to the money," Jaelen said. "We take what they love the most, family, and make them choose."

"That one bitch don't have any kids.

As for their husbands, they don't give a fuck about them. If they did, they wouldn't have been fucking with you," Monty said. "How would they know to move as they did and when they did?"

Both Monty and SK looked on at Jaelen checking to see if he was slipping and somehow falling for one of these women.

"My end was secured from day one. Don't think I slipped up," Jaelen said.

"We're the only ones, standing right here, to know that we were taking the money before Tuesday. I know I didn't say shit," SK snapped, still holding his gun in hand. Right then, angered by this total loss of trust and control, Jaelen snapped and charged toward SK, tussling with him until the gun was knocked from his grasp. They fell on the floor by the coffee table, where SK was holding Jaelen down trying to choke him out. At the same time, Jaelen saw it: a wiretap underneath the coffee table. The only other female he had allowed into his home other than Laila was Danna. Laila came after they discussed this matter of taking the money. They were listening in every time he and his associates met at the condo. Jaelen flipped SK off of him and away long enough to speak.

"They planted a bug under the coffee table!" he let out, breathing heavily and flipping the table, taking the electronic device off. "It was that Asian bitch, Danna. She was the only one in my place before Laila." He handed it to Monty.

"This isn't cheap. They must know someone that can get them this type of device," Monty said.

"They are going need to know someone if they don't get our fucking money back," SK said.

"We need money to travel, fools," Jaelen said.

"Don't tell me you dummies don't have a go bag?" Monty said, knowing in this business you have to have a go bag, in case of emergencies like now. The bag contained $100,000, a gun, passports, a quick makeshift disguise, two burner cell phones, and keys to a car parked outside of the city.

"We don't think that far ahead like you, being a genius," SK said.

"Since you two are done fighting each other, let's go. I'll finance this chase to get our money back. They have a jump on us. The only advantage we have is knowing where they're going. We'll fly directly to Dubai and land a day before them. This will give us a chance to try to find the bank or banks where they may have placed the money," Monty said.

Jaelen rushed back into the bedroom and got his clothing on before they all headed out to the car and raced to the airport.

The ladies had gotten away with Tanya's money and their spouses' money, as well as Jaelen, Monty and

SK's money, totaling $68 million they would comfortably split after getting lost around the globe.

NINE

Monday 3:45 p.m. Middle Eastern
Time over in Dubai.

Jaelen along with his associates were
at the international airport sitting in the
all-white Mercedes Benz S600L rental
behind the dark tinted windows to blend
in with the affluent lifestyle this country

offered global celebrities, millionaires, and billionaires who called this country their playground. It made sense for the ladies to have their money sent here, because to those from this country $68 million is what most billionaires blow on their loved ones in the way of yachts, islands, or private jets. As for Jaelen and his crew, $68 million to them was a billion dollars, especially now, not having anything but what they had in the go bag and other properties they had and no cash or money in their banks.

"Their plane should have landed by now," SK said, becoming impatient and wanting to get to these women so he could get his money back.

"If they have luggage, they have to get it," Jaelen said.

"I doubt they would have luggage, being in a hurry as they were," Monty said, looking on at his laptop and trying to retrace the money that had left their accounts. Still nothing.

As they were waiting, a convoy pulled up. Two all-white G500 Mercedes Benz trucks followed behind an all-white Maybach S67L with the curtains drawn concealing its passengers. As the vehicles all came to a halt, two men from each of the trucks exited in black two-piece suits looking to be security for whoever was in the Maybach or coming to get into the Maybach. Two of the men stood close by the Maybach while the others remained by the outside of the trucks.

"What, they got a prince or something coming?" SK said.

"Not likely," Monty replied before adding, "anyone with royal status would fly into the private airports as a respectful gesture to their guest. Also, because they can afford to fly on private jets."

Jaelen could care less about those cars. He was focused on the exits looking for Danna and Paula, wanting his money. He didn't even care why they had done it, since their reasoning wouldn't add value to anything. As he was locked on the door, he briefly flashed back to the first time Danna came to his place and how it all happened with her acting as if she had locked her keys in the car. He later discovered she lied when Monty said there weren't any keys locked in. Her being at his place explained the bug, but what got him was Paula, what was her reasoning in being persistent in coming on to him? He questioned himself trying to go over every little detail. His thoughts came to an abrupt halt when he heard SK in the back seat.

"There them bitches go right there!" he said, seeing them exit the airport smiling. "You hoes ain't going to be smiling for too long," he added.

"How do you want to handle this, Jaelen?" Monty asked, watching the ladies, luggage-free, walking past the other cars and making their way over to the convoy they noticed. Each of the women walked to the back of the Maybach that rolled its back window down partially. They were smiling at the person in the back seat. The women stood there for another thirty seconds smiling and nodding their heads in their brief conversation with whoever was in the back seat of the Maybach. The window rolled up on the Maybach. At the same time the two men on the outside of the car guided the women to the trucks. Both of them got into the back seat of the first truck. Once inside, the trucks followed behind the Maybach.

"Follow them muthafuckas wherever

they go," SK said.

"They're going to lead us right to the money, no doubt. This is why they came here," Monty said as Jaelen drove off following behind the trucks.

Close to twenty minutes passed before they were pulling up to a five-diamond resort owned by Kari Abdul Shakur, an oil tycoon who enjoyed global investments, as this resort boasted one hundred floors, a sky lounge, and an infinity pool for the views of the skyline. It also had indoor waterfalls and five-star dining, having the best chefs in the world working around the clock to cater to his elite clientele, royalty and billionaires. Each guest also had access to the resort's fleet of Maybachs, Bentleys, Rolls Royces and other imported cars to appease their sumptuous desires.

Jaelen, along with SK and Monty, was becoming anxious, wanting to confront both women to get their money.

The trucks and Maybach halted at the entrance, the valets being prompt and racing over to the vehicles opening the doors.

"Get out so we can check these

bitches," SK said, opening his door and jumping out. The valet came over to their car figuring they too were guests.

"Welcome to the Imperial Palace," the valet said.

Each of them exited the car at the same time and saw Danna and Paula all dressed up and happy as ever having stolen their money.

The women were so focused walking toward the Maybach they didn't notice the men approaching.

The door to the Maybach opened at the same time the security halted Jaelen and his associates, seeing they were walking too fast toward their clients.

When the passenger in the Maybach exited, it took Jaelen, Monty, and SK by surprise. Each of them felt the ultimate betrayal of being deceived as Laila exited looking like a billionaire's daughter adjusting her Versace shades. What caught her attention to the men at her right were her security pointing them out to her.

"Ms. Patrones, do you know these men?"

She turned, shocked to see them

here, just as Danna and Paula were.

"You bitches stole our money!" SK blurted out.

"Laila, this is how you going to play me?" Jaelen snapped, feeling a total loss of control.

She removed her shades looking on at Jaelen. A part of her wanted him to be in on this, but he had made his decision the night she posed the question to him. His actions were the opposite.

"I asked you what was more important to you, the prize or the reward? So I don't regret my decision. I only regret you won't be able to enjoy this new life with me I wanted with you so much," she said, placing her shades back on at the same time hotel security came out, being made aware that a problem was arising.

"Mrs. Patrones, is everything fine here?" the security head said with six of his men at his arms with weapons concealed to give respect to their elite customers.

"Yes, my lady friends and I were just heading up to our suites to celebrate. As for these men, they were just leaving," she responded.

"Bitch, you going to give me my money!" SK snapped. She didn't even look his way as she was escorted into the hotel by the security along with Danna and Paula, who didn't even want to look at Jaelen after their betrayal. The security surrounded Jaelen and his friends and forced them back into the car.

For the first time they all were feeling defeated.

"We didn't fly this far for nothing, Jaelen. We have to get our money back from them bitches!" SK said, full of anger, not wanting to go back to the United

States until he got his money—nothing more or less. They didn't realize this business they were in came with the pros and cons of being a con artist. They got played at what they did best. Now they either had to tuck their tails and head back to the States and start all over, or try to figure something out. Right now, Laila had the upper hand of knowing they were here to get their money, so she had to think faster and smarter to protect herself and the money.

TEN

Two miles down the road Jaelen pulled over and got out of the car as if a bright light of ideas had hit him.

"I got it. I got it. They want to play, we'll play," he said, walking back and forth. Monty and SK exited the car, seeing their associate pacing.

"Are you going to fill us in on the bright idea you have bottled up?" Monty asked. Jaelen halted, looking over at Monty.

"It's game time, Monty. We may have to grease a few palms to make this work, but we have sixty-eight million reasons to go all in on this one," Jaelen said, getting back into the car, driving, and telling them his ideas. If it didn't work, it'd be a long way home.

8:13 p.m.

The ladies were just returning from dinner on their lower level of the resort. Each of them were laughing and feeling good about this new life they had of being single and rich. They entered the elevator and took it back to their suite on the 80th floor.

Jaelen had been the topic over dinner and how he treated each woman emotionally and sexually. Laila didn't want to hear this; however, the tricks he imposed on each woman intrigued her because his approach to her was different. This meant he had more to offer that she would never get a chance to experience. Once in the elevator, the conversation shifted to money, business and where everyone would go after tonight.

"First thing in the morning we'll head to the bank. We'll have them draw up three separate checks to divide the money. After that, you ladies will head back to the airport and to the destination of your choice. I'm sure there's going to be another Jaelen somewhere in the world to appease your sexual cravings," Laila said.

"What about you? You're not going anywhere?" Danna asked.

"I'm flying out the following day," Laila responded as the doors to their elevator opened.

They headed back to the suite. Laila could see the dozens of assorted roses on the floor at the door's entrance. This made her look around, knowing the only person that would want to send her flowers was Jalen. What was he up to? She had to stay ahead of him and get as far away from him as possible. She knew this because the closer he was to her, the more likely he was going to figure something out to make him preeminent in the end.

"Somebody thinks we're special sending roses," Paula said.

"Not we, me," Laila said, seeing the card with her name on it. She leaned down and took the card while Danna picked the roses up and smelled them. She opened the card that read: "Sometimes you have to endure the pain to enjoy the pleasure that follows."

She read it to herself before passing it to the others to see what they make of it before she overreacted. It didn't take a genius to know who it was from. She opened the door to the suite looking around to see if he or his crazy-ass friends were in here, since they somehow had managed to get the flowers here. Laila knew for the amount of money they had taken, he and his friends would stop at nothing. She feared being harmed, killed even. Little did she know Jaelen and Monty weren't that type. She should be more worried about SK, who would kill her without question for the sixty-eight million. Nothing and no one was inside. She rushed over to her things and checked her laptop, turning it on to see if there had been any activity on it. Nothing. She felt good knowing no one had been inside her suite.

"Tomorrow can't come fast enough, ladies." Laila said, wanting to physically secure the money in the form of a check, instead of on her laptop, which could be compromised if accessed.

"That was him with the roses and card?" Danna asked. "I don't want to die over this," she said sounding scared, thinking about the life she had run away from to this life on the run from the people she stole the money from.

"No one is going to die. At least I don't think so. Don't worry, we'll all have our money in the morning as soon as the banks open. By the time they wake up we'll have what we came for. Then we all can vanish. Now grab that bottle over there so we can celebrate to this good life we all deserve," Laila responded. Deep inside she was anxious, in need of this drink to calm her nerves.

The ladies found themselves drinking shot after shot while standing at the floor-to-ceiling window looking out at the view from the 80th floor of the suite. The starlit skyline was accompanied by the back light of the moon. The other towering hotels and resorts added to the art of this picturesque sight. The new life of single millionaires.

"No one is going to take this moment from us, or this life we went through so much to obtain," Laila said.

"We all had fun with him in our own way. It felt good, but these millions and this view right here feel a lot better," Paula said, drinking her shot. "Pour me another."

Laila didn't say a word. She was too focused on keep her riches, knowing as long as their money remained in the back for the next twelve hours until opening, she wouldn't have a good night sleep or have clear thoughts.

Almost two hours passed by with the ladies drinking, laughing, and reminiscing in detail about Jaelen, and planning their new future, when a knock came across the door shifting the mood as well as their attention.

"Did you two order anything?" Laila asked.

"No, I didn't," Paula responded.

"Me neither, but I am hungry," Danna added.

Laila stood and made her way to the door. When she made it to the door and looked through the peephole, she saw resort staff standing there. She opened the door.

"Hello, Ms. Patrones. You have a guest who insisted on delivering his message personally," the staff said. At the same time Jaelen came from the left into clear view. She sucked in a breath of disbelief backed by fear hoping he didn't come to kill her.

"You win, beautiful, so why be bitter about it?" he said, bringing forward a jewelry box and extending it to her. He wanted her to feel at ease and calm and not be afraid of him. He never welcomed this type of fear. Laila was looking on at the gift box hesitating to take it, looking down at it then back up to him searching his eyes to see if they matched his gift. She extended her hand to take the gift, and he brought his other hand up caressing her hand as she took hold of the gift. His touch reminded her of how passionate he was. "Open it."

She did just that revealing a diamond necklace with a yellow, white, and blue diamond butterfly the size of a fifty-cent piece coming alive as if it was a real butterfly the way it was sparking. A part of her wanted to welcome him in to show her appreciation. The other part, being smart, wanted to protect her girls and interest, which was the money.

"Thank you. It's beautiful."

"Not as beautiful as you are inside and out. Besides, you won and you deserve it. It best represents the rare person and beauty you possess," he said, turning to walk away, leaving her with the gift and his words to hold onto forever. So many thoughts raced through her head wanting what they had to work, but he chose the money over her, which forced her decision. She stood in the doorway hoping he would look back or say something that would make her want to run away and share all with him, but nothing. She closed the door and headed back into the suite over to the women.

"Who was that?" Danna asked.

"A gift from a friend of ours," Laila responded, displaying the gift.

"He's really heartbroken," Paula said. "Sorry not sorry for the million-dollar single life." They all laughed.

"It's beautiful and it's mine now," Laila said, placing the necklace around her neck. The clarity, cut, and colors all made it sparkle from every direction the light was hitting it.

Their night came to an end with a few more drinks and plans before each of them found their beds and dozed off into a deep sleep.

ELEVEN

7:58 a.m.

Laila and the girls were all arriving at the Vartan International Bank of Dubai in three separate Maybachs provided by the resort to take them where they pleased. Each of them exited their vehicles and made their way up the steps of the bank. They were immediately greeted by the doorman.

"Good morning, ladies. Welcome to the Vartan International Bank. We appreciate your services," he said, scanning his key card over the eight-ball-like bulb that illuminated blue acknowledging his card. A beeping sound came before the vaulted doors released a swish of air and the doors opened. The doorman continued smiling as he waved the women past.

Jaelen, SK, and Monty were less than

one hundred yards away ready to make their move yet watching the ladies closely.

7:59:49 is what it read on Monty's computer screen.

"In eleven seconds, we'll know if we're going home broke or rich," Monty said, now having the account numbers and the bank, thanks to Jaelen's genius idea of placing the transmitter into the necklace he gave Laila as a gift, knowing she wouldn't trust him showing up, and would continue to check her account through the night. In doing this she allowed Monty to gain access to her account numbers. All they needed now was the bank to open up for business so they too could secure the check.

8:00 a.m.

Jaelen looked down at his watch and saw the time, ready to put into play his most deceptive move to date.

"It's time," he said. SK pulled off, racing up to the front of the bank so Jaelen could make his move.

"You should have this all done by the time I walk in asking for the check," Jaelen said, exiting the car looking like a successful millionaire wearing his white Armani two-piece suit with red cotton Ralph Lauren shirt underneath, platinum cuff links, and white Versace framed shades, all flowing with his Ralph Lauren blood-red leather shoes. He entered the bank bypassing the ladies unseen and was greeted by the bank's manager, who was expecting him after he made an abrupt call stating there was a numbers difference in his account far from what his accountant had. This prompted the bank's staff to get on this right away, since their name was on the line.

"Mr. Santiago, right this way. I'm quite

sorry for you having to come here on such occasion. I assure you everything is in order just as you requested. The numbers are all in order," the manager said, gesturing for Jaelen to have a seat. "Asiento por favor," the manager said, asking him to be seated. The manager was able to speak multiple languages, having the need to with the global clientele base.

"I'll stand, yo solo quiero mi chabo," Jaelen said, making the manager feel a need to please him since he spoke saying he only wanted his money.

"One second, I can have it printed out right now," he said, running his fingers across the keys on his computer to access the account. He could see the amount of a little over sixty-eight million, since the ladies splurged yesterday with the suite costing fifty thousand a night plus all of the things they purchased while in the room. "Here we go," he said, printing the check out and handing it to Jaelen. He wasn't out of the clear, yet he needed to get out of the bank without the ladies noticing him, knowing if they caused a scene no one would get the money. This could take weeks, months or years, depending on how good their staff was.

"Gracious, mi amigo. I will recommend this place to my associates now that I see that the numbers you have are very accurate. On the other hand, I will be firing my accountant for having me go through so much trouble," Jaelen said, shaking the manager's hand before turning around to leave. As he exited the office, he could hear the voices of Laila, Danna, and Paula, their tones climbing a notch now realizing there was no money in their accounts. Jaelen continued walking, making his way out of the bank over to the rented S600L Mercedes Benz. At the same time his cell phone sounded off. Still in character, he spoke in Spanish. "Hola que tal?"

"Jaelen," a soft voice came across the phone sounding helpless and in need. It was Laila. "You win. You won my heart, my body, my mind, and the money. I love you. Please don't do this." She was pleading knowing somehow she would have to find her way back to the United States along with Danna and Paula, having no money and having to explain to their husbands where the money was. Jaelen wasn't buying her emotional plea no matter how sincere it was. In fact, the power of being in control now with the money and being over her and the three women simultaneously gave him his confidence back. "I always win," he said, hanging up the phone and tossing it into the trash outside of the bank before entering the car. SK pulled off blending into the traffic. At the same time the women all came outside looking outside to see if they could spot Jaelen, knowing he's close.

Jaelen pulled the checkout feeling much better than he was before.

"Thanks to all of our creative genius, we're back."

"Does this mean we're going to Brazil or what?" SK asked.

"The way I'm feeling having this check right here, we can go anywhere," Jaelen responded.

"Brazil is not a bad place to chill for a few months," Monty said. "We need the time off."

"I'm done. We'll split this paper we profited, but I'm out," Jaelen said.

"Say no more. Just let me enjoy the bikini and thong life in Brazil. I'm good,"

SK said.

Monty didn't want it to all come to an end. They were good at what they did, but every day had its meaning and own events. This lifestyle they were living had come to an end.

"I'm with you on this, bro. We came, we saw, we conquered," Monty said before leaning back, closing his laptop, and staring out the window at the beautiful and sumptuous Dubai.

EPILOUGE

Two weeks later down in Brazil, Jaelen, Monty, and SK were all enjoying the good life at the beach villa they had rented out. It boasted views of the ocean crashing up on the sands coupled with countless exotic-looking women wearing bikinis and some in the nude feeling comfortable in their skin. Each of the men sat back with their feet in the sand sipping mixed drinks, circled by these foreign women who were enjoying every bit of their American ways. It felt good to them not being in the game of deception that made them rich, but enjoying the spoils of it, or so they thought, until unexpected mail came.

"Senor Jones, I have a package for you," the mail carrier yelled out from the beach villa seeing they were surrounded by beautiful women. Jaelen looked over his shoulder at the carrier, then back to his associates.

"Did one of you order something to be mailed here?" Jaelen questioned.

"Everything I need is right here. Ain't that right, Fernanda?" SK asked said, tapping her ass.

"Si, papi chulo," she responded, smiling and leaning in sip out of his mixed drink.

"Whatever it is, tell them we don't want it," Monty said, enjoying the company of the Brazilian women.

Jaelen headed over to the mail carrier and signed for the large envelope. The carrier left, leaving him to view the contents of the envelope. Jaelen opened it and removed the Samsung tablet, turning it on curious to know who sent it. As soon as it came on, he could see Danna's sad eyes and bruised face. Right then he knew something was very wrong. "Please don't hurt me. I have kids. I don't have the money," she pleaded. At the same time a gun came into view pressing up against her head. Then it happened: the gunman fired a round into her head, jolting Jaelen and making him jump back as if he was in the room and was next.

"What the fuck was that?" he said,

shaken by what he just had seen yet unable to look away as the cameraman moved to Paula, who was looking beat up and bloody. "No, no, no, please, I don't have the money." Her eyes showed the fear of death, and the gun appeared in view and fired into her face, slumping her right there. It definitely wasn't worth their lives either. The camera shifted to a screaming Laila.

"Oh God, please don't let this happen to me. I'm sorry, please."

To order books, please fill out the order form below:

To order films please go to www.good2gofilms.com

Name:_____

Address:_____

City:_____State:_____Zip Code: _____

Phone:_____

Email:_____

Method of Payment: Check   VISA MASTERCARD

Credit Card#:_ _____

Name as it appears on card: _____

Signature: _____

Item Name	Price	Qty	Amount
48 Hours to Die – Silk White	$14.99		
A Hustler's Dream – Ernest Morris	$14.99		
A Hustler's Dream 2 – Ernest Morris	$14.99		
A Thug's Devotion – J. L. Rose and J. M. McMillon	$14.99		
All Eyes on Tommy Gunz – Warren Holloway	$14.99		
Black Reign – Ernest Morris	$14.99		
Bloody Mayhem Down South – Trayvon Jackson	$14.99		
Bloody Mayhem Down South 2 – Trayvon Jackson	$14.99		
Business Is Business – Silk White	$14.99		
Business Is Business 2 – Silk White	$14.99		
Business Is Business 3 – Silk White	$14.99		
Cash In Cash Out – Assa Raymond Baker	$14.99		
Cash In Cash Out 2 – Assa Raymond Baker	$14.99		
Childhood Sweethearts – Jacob Spears	$14.99		
Childhood Sweethearts 2 – Jacob Spears	$14.99		
Childhood Sweethearts 3 – Jacob Spears	$14.99		
Childhood Sweethearts 4 – Jacob Spears	$14.99		
Connected To The Plug – Dwan Marquis Williams	$14.99		
Connected To The Plug 2 – Dwan Marquis Williams	$14.99		
Connected To The Plug 3 – Dwan Williams	$14.99		
Cost of Betrayal – W.C. Holloway	$14.99		
Cost of Betrayal 2 – W.C. Holloway	$14.99		
Deadly Reunion – Ernest Morris	$14.99		
Dream's Life – Assa Raymond Baker	$14.99		
Flipping Numbers – Ernest Morris	$14.99		

Item Name	Price	Qty	Amount
Flipping Numbers 2 – Ernest Morris	$14.99		
He Loves Me, He Loves You Not – Mychea	$14.99		
He Loves Me, He Loves You Not 2 – Mychea	$14.99		
He Loves Me, He Loves You Not 3 – Mychea	$14.99		
He Loves Me, He Loves You Not 4 – Mychea	$14.99		
He Loves Me, He Loves You Not 5 – Mychea	$14.99		
Killing Signs – Ernest Morris	$14.99		
Killing Signs 2 – Ernest Morris	$14.99		
Kings of the Block – Dwan Willams	$14.99		
Kings of the Block 2 – Dwan Willams	$14.99		
Lord of My Land – Jay Morrison	$14.99		
Lost and Turned Out – Ernest Morris	$14.99		
Love & Dedication – W.C. Holloway	$14.99		
Love Hates Violence – De'Wayne Maris	$14.99		
Love Hates Violence 2 – De'Wayne Maris	$14.99		
Love Hates Violence 3 – De'Wayne Maris	$14.99		
Love Hates Violence 4 – De'Wayne Maris	$14.99		
Married To Da Streets – Silk White	$14.99		
M.E.R.C. – Make Every Rep Count Health and Fitness	$14.99		
Mercenary In Love – J.L. Rose & J.L. Turner	$14.99		
Money Make Me Cum – Ernest Morris	$14.99		
My Besties – Asia Hill	$14.99		
My Besties 2 – Asia Hill	$14.99		
My Besties 3 – Asia Hill	$14.99		
My Besties 4 – Asia Hill	$14.99		
My Boyfriend's Wife – Mychea	$14.99		
My Boyfriend's Wife 2 – Mychea	$14.99		
My Brothers Envy – J. L. Rose	$14.99		
My Brothers Envy 2 – J. L. Rose	$14.99		
Naughty Housewives – Ernest Morris	$14.99		
Naughty Housewives 2 – Ernest Morris	$14.99		
Naughty Housewives 3 – Ernest Morris	$14.99		
Naughty Housewives 4 – Ernest Morris	$14.99		
Never Be The Same – Silk White	$14.99		

Item Name	Price	Qty	Amount
Scarred Faces – Assa Raymond Baker	$14.99		
Scarred Knuckles – Assa Raymond Baker	$14.99		
Shades of Revenge – Assa Raymond Baker	$14.99		
Slumped – Jason Brent	$14.99		
Someone's Gonna Get It – Mychea	$14.99		
Stranded – Silk White	$14.99		
Supreme & Justice – Ernest Morris	$14.99		
Supreme & Justice 2 – Ernest Morris	$14.99		
Supreme & Justice 3 – Ernest Morris	$14.99		
Tears of a Hustler – Silk White	$14.99		
Tears of a Hustler 2 – Silk White	$14.99		
Tears of a Hustler 3 – Silk White	$14.99		
Tears of a Hustler 4– Silk White	$14.99		
Tears of a Hustler 5 – Silk White	$14.99		
Tears of a Hustler 6 – Silk White	$14.99		
The Excitement I Bring – Warren Holloway	$14.99		
The Excitement I Bring 2 – Warren Holloway	$14.99		
The Last Love Letter – Warren Holloway	$14.99		
The Last Love Letter 2 – Warren Holloway	$14.99		
The Panty Ripper – Reality Way	$14.99		
The Panty Ripper 3 – Reality Way	$14.99		
The Solution – Jay Morrison	$14.99		
The Teflon Queen – Silk White	$14.99		
The Teflon Queen 2 – Silk White	$14.99		
The Teflon Queen 3 – Silk White	$14.99		
The Teflon Queen 4 – Silk White	$14.99		
The Teflon Queen 5 – Silk White	$14.99		
The Teflon Queen 6 – Silk White	$14.99		
The Vacation – Silk White	$14.99		
Tied To A Boss – J.L. Rose	$14.99		
Tied To A Boss 2 – J.L. Rose	$14.99		
Tied To A Boss 3 – J.L. Rose	$14.99		
Tied To A Boss 4 – J.L. Rose	$14.99		
Tied To A Boss 5 – J.L. Rose	$14.99		
Time Is Money – Silk White	$14.99		

Item Name	Price	Qty	Amount
Tomorrow's Not Promised – Robert Torres	$14.99		
Tomorrow's Not Promised 2 – Robert Torres	$14.99		
Two Mask One Heart – Jacob Spears and Trayvon Jackson	$14.99		
Two Mask One Heart 2 – Jacob Spears and Trayvon Jackson	$14.99		
Two Mask One Heart 3 – Jacob Spears and Trayvon Jackson	$14.99		
Wrong Place Wrong Time – Silk White	$14.99		
Young Goonz – Reality Way	$14.99		
Subtotal:			
Tax:			
Shipping (Free) U.S. Media Mail:			
Total:			

Make Checks Payable To: Good2Go Publishing, 7311 W Glass Lane, Laveen, AZ 85339